# Monkey and the White Bone Demon

# MONKEY AND THE WHITE BONE DEMON

Adapted by Zhang Xiu Shi from the novel, *The Pilgrimage to the West*, by Wu Cheng En

Illustrated by Lin Zheng, Fei Chang Fu, Xin Kuan Liang and Zhang Xiu Shi

Translated by Ye Ping Kuei and revised by Jill Morris

## Kestrel Books
## The Viking Press

Published in association with Liaoning Fine Arts Publishing House, China

Kestrel Books
Published by Penguin Books Australia Ltd.,
487 Maroondah Highway
Ringwood, Victoria, Australia
Penguin Books Ltd
Harmondsworth, Middlesex, England

First published in association with Liaoning Fine Arts Publishing House, China, 1984
Illustrations copyright © Lin Zheng, Fei Chang Fu, Xin Kuan Liang and
Zhang Xiu Shi, 1984
Text copyright © Ye Ping Kue and Jill Morris, 1984

**CIP**

Zhang, Xiu Shi.
Monkey and the white bone demon.
For children.
ISBN 0 7226 5928 8.
I. Wu, Ch'êng ên, ca. 1500-ca. 1582. Hsi yu chi.
II. Lin, Zheng. III. Ye, Ping Kuei. IV. Morris
Jill. V. Title. VI. Title: Hsi yu chi.
895.1'35

Viking US ISBN 0-670-48574-8
Library of Congress Cataloging in Publication Data
Morris, Jill.
Monkey and the White Bone Demon.
Based on one episode of Hsi yu chi/Wu Ch'eng-en.
Summary: While he is traveling to the Western Heaven
in quest of the ancient Buddhist scriptures, the monk
Hsuan Tsang is captured by the White Bone Demon and his
disciple Monkey tries to rescue him.
[1. Folklore—China] I. Wu, Ch'eng en, ca. 1500-ca.
1582. Hsi yu chi. II. Title.
PZ8.1.M8285Mo 1984    398.2'1'0951 [E]    83-17670
ISBN 0-670-48574-8

Printed and bound in Singapore by Tien Wah Press

Designed by George Dale

The monk Hsuan Tsang was on his way to the Western Heaven in quest of the ancient Buddhist scriptures. With him were his disciples – Monkey, Pigsy and Sandy – and Monkey was leading the way.

After a long journey they reached a barren mountain. They were very tired and hungry but Monkey sensed danger and decided to go on ahead. With his gold-tipped staff he traced a magic circle around his friends. 'Don't step out of this circle for anyone. I don't want you to be devoured by monsters,' he warned them before he somersaulted away.

Deep in the mountain, ruling over a band of evil spirits, lived the fearsome White Bone Demon who could change herself into any disguise. Hearing that the monk Hsuan Tsang had arrived, she set out to capture him.

The White Bone Demon discovered Hsuan Tsang and his two disciples, sitting inside Monkey's magic circle, deep in meditation. There was no Monkey to defend them.

Delighted with her good fortune, the White Bone Demon tried to attack Hsuan Tsang but the golden rays of Monkey's circle drove her back.

Not giving up, the Demon disguised herself as a young girl, carrying a basket of steamed buns.

The aroma of the buns woke Pigsy and he stepped out of the magic circle.

'Food' he shouted. 'That smells good!' But the young girl was moving away.

'Where are you going?' he asked her.

'To the temple,' she replied enticingly.

'Then we're going too. Come on Master!' And ignoring Monkey's instructions, Pigsy dragged Hsuan Tsang out of the magic circle which had been protecting him.

Suddenly Monkey jumped in front of them. 'Wicked Monster!' he screamed, and killed the girl with his staff.

He knew she was the White Bone Demon in disguise.

As the body of the girl fell to the ground, the White Bone Demon escaped from it in a wisp of cloud. Hsuan Tsang was horrified at Monkey's violence. 'It is a crime to kill,' he cried.

But Monkey had already taken off in hot pursuit.

Knowing that Monkey was missing, the White Bone Demon
reappeared – this time as an old woman.

'What have you done with my daughter?' she croaked, grasping the monk
by the arm. 'Justice will be done and her death will be avenged.'

But Monkey had somersaulted back. He slashed at the old woman with his staff, while his three companions watched, horrified. But again the Demon escaped, in a wisp of cloud, from the body of the old woman.

'You wicked Disciple!' Hsuan Tsang hissed at Monkey. 'Don't you know it is a crime to kill all living creatures?'

Next, the White Bone Demon came disguised as an old man, in mourning for his daughter and his wife. 'What have you done with my old companion?' he rasped through his beard.

But when Monkey swung his staff to kill the old man, Hsuan Tsang cried out,' You devil! You've already killed a mother and her daughter. I'm not going to let you destroy this one.'

'Out of my way, Master!' screamed Monkey. 'This monster may be able to change her shape, but her nature will never change.' And he knocked the old man over the cliff to the rocks below.

Monkey was about to pursue the demon spirit when a cloud appeared in the sky and a scroll of yellow silk floated from it and settled at the feet of Hsuan Tsang.

The monk picked it up and read: 'Buddha is full of compassion and will never tolerate killing. You will never find the Heavenly Scriptures as long as Monkey remains in your entourage.'

Believing the message came from the Buddha, Hsuan Tsang ordered Monkey to return to his home on Fruit and Flower Mountain – despite the pleas of Sandy and Pigsy to let him remain.

Monkey bade a sad farewell to his friends and with one super somersault returned to his home.

Despondently, the three travellers continued on their way. At dusk,
just as they were looking for shelter, a temple rose before them.
'First we must pay homage to Buddha,' said the monk, and they went in.

Hsuan Tsang knelt and prayed before the giant Buddha. 'Bless us, O Lord. Grant us a safe journey and help us find the Heavenly Scriptures.'

But the giant Buddha laughed. 'You fool! You stupid monk! You can't tell truth from falsehood. You've stumbled right into my lair!'
And then the Buddha turned into the White Bone Demon and the other buddhas became her demon disciples.

The evil spirits seized Hsuan Tsang and though Pigsy and Sandy fought bravely to protect him, they were surrounded on all sides.

Sandy was taken prisoner, but Pigsy managed to break free. He hurried to Monkey's home on Fruit and Flower Mountain.
Monkey was relaxing, very much at home.

'Monkey, come back and save the Master,' pleaded Pigsy. 'He needs you.'

But Monkey shook his head. 'As Master is so smart, let him persuade the White Bone Demon to let him go free.'

'All right. If that's the way you feel about it, I'll fight the White Bone Demon on my own, until my last breath.' And Pigsy lumbered away in a huff.

As soon as Pigsy had disappeared, Monkey bounded on to a cloud and streaked off, headed for the White Bone Demon's cave. But on his way he spied the Golden Toad Fairy, mother of the White Bone Demon, who had been invited to feast on the flesh of Hsuan Tsang.

She was on her way to her daughter's cave, accompanied by all the demons of her household.

Wielding his staff, Monkey descended from the clouds and slaughtered the Golden Toad Fairy, destroying all her demons with her.

Plucking hairs from his body, Monkey transformed each hair into a likeness of himself. Then he turned himself into the form of the Golden Toad Fairy and all the other monkeys into her demons – and they all continued their procession to the White Bone Demon's cave.

Meanwhile, Pigsy had also been captured and was waiting trussed and fettered in the White Bone Demon's cave, ready to be roasted when the Golden Toad Fairy came.

At last the Fairy (Monkey in disguise) arrived at her daughter's cave. 'What a clever daughter you are! All those delicious offerings waiting over there. I'm delighted that you invited me,' she said.

'Tell me daughter,' asked the Golden Toad (Monkey), 'how did you
entice Hsuan Tsang into your cave?'

'It was easy,' the Demon cooed. 'I just changed into three shapes – first
a young girl, then an old woman, and finally an old man. But Monkey saw
through all my disguises and conquered them all. So then I dropped a
scroll from Heaven, instructing the monk to send Monkey away.'

'I've been deceived!' gasped Hsuan Tsang, only now realizing the truth. 'If only I'd listened to Monkey! If only I'd learned to distinguish between right and wrong, between friend and foe!'

But then the Golden Toad Fairy cried out, with Monkey's voice, 'It's all right, Master. Monkey is here!'

And the Golden Toad Fairy was gone...

And Monkey. . .Monkey was everywhere. Clones of Monkey, making sure that the White Bone Demon would be captured, whichever way she ran.

Spitting out magic flames, Monkey at last reduced the Demon to her true form – a pile of whitened bones.

Afterwards, Hsuan Tsang was ashamed. 'It was my fault, Monkey. I mistook the evil ones for innocents.'

'Monsters are like that, Master,' said Monkey. 'They are here to bring death and misfortune to man. There'll be more of them on our way to the West. We'll have to be on our guard.'

And so the four travellers continued their journey to the Western Heavens, with Monkey leading the way.